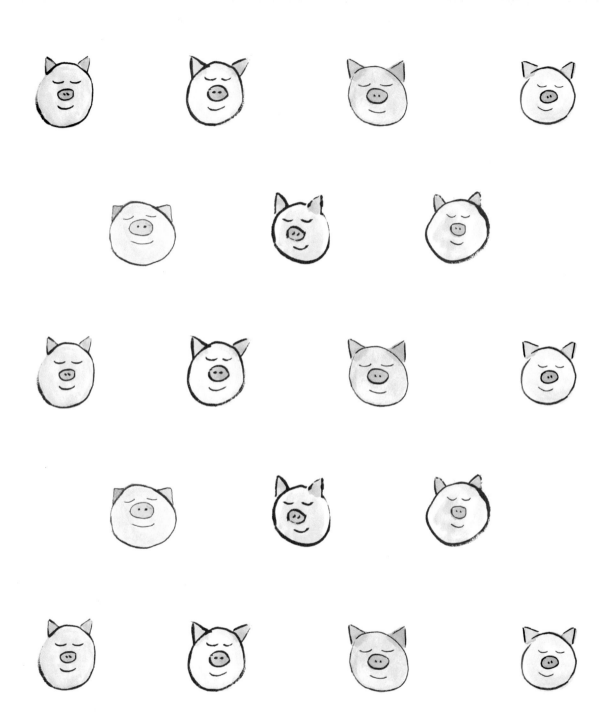

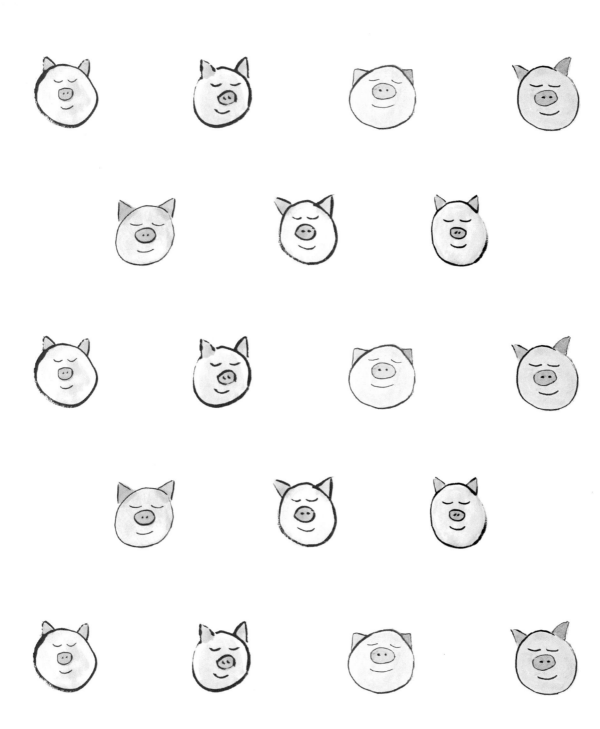

Zen Pig

Book 8

The 7 Rules of Valentine's Day

written by:

mark brown

illustrated by:

mariangela cinelli

Spread the love with...
#ZenPig

Dedicated to all fellow light bearers.

Now, more than ever,
the world needs
your unique good.

Stay relentlessly positive.

Bright and early, Zen Pig awoke,
As he did this day each year.
Valentine's Day was here again,
And it was time to spread some cheer.

With joy, Zen Pig put on his best,
Grabbed his things, and was on his way.
Headed to town to spread his love,
On this very special day.

Two sad bears on his route,
Made Zen Pig come to a stop.
He asked them, "What's the matter?
What's made your faces drop?"

"Nobody loves us…"
The pair did sadly say.
"We've not a single Valentine
After here waiting all day."

"Come with me," Zen Pig began,
"There are many who feel the same.
But they just don't know the seven rules
Of the Valentine's Day game."

Rule #1

"Rule number one," Zen Pig started,
"Is simple yet often forgotten,
The score is kept by how much love you give,
Never by how much is gotten.

Rule #2

Rule number two
Might be easiest of them all,
Thinking of love as just cards and kisses
Is to see love much too small.

Rule #3

The next one to remember
Is that love is not spoken, but shown.
Through our actions and behavior
Is how our feelings are known.

Rule #4

Even with three rules down,
You may be asking where to begin.
Rule four is to show love to yourself,
Love must always start from within.

Rule #5

To honor love and its power
You'll find is rule number five.
It heals, transforms, and nurtures.
It is the only way to thrive.

Rule #6

There is no life without love.
That's rule number six.
Happiness and a hollow heart
Simply do not mix.

Rule #7

Lastly, learn to accept,
Not reject the gift of love.
Many don't feel worthy of it,
But it's something we're all deserving of.

Just then, they turned the corner

And found themselves back at the start.

Their once empty bags were now overflowing,

Now that the lessons were in their heart.

Namaste.

("The light in me loves the light in you.")

Zen Pig's 7 Valentine's Day Rules

1. Count how much love you GIVE, not how much you receive.

2. Love means more than hugs and kisses. Kindness, acknowledgment, and gratitude are all forms of love.

3. Love is not spoken. Love is shown.

4. Love must always start within ourselves.

5. Everyone needs love to grow.

6. Love must be a priority to have a happy life.

7. Learning to accept love is a skill that we must learn.

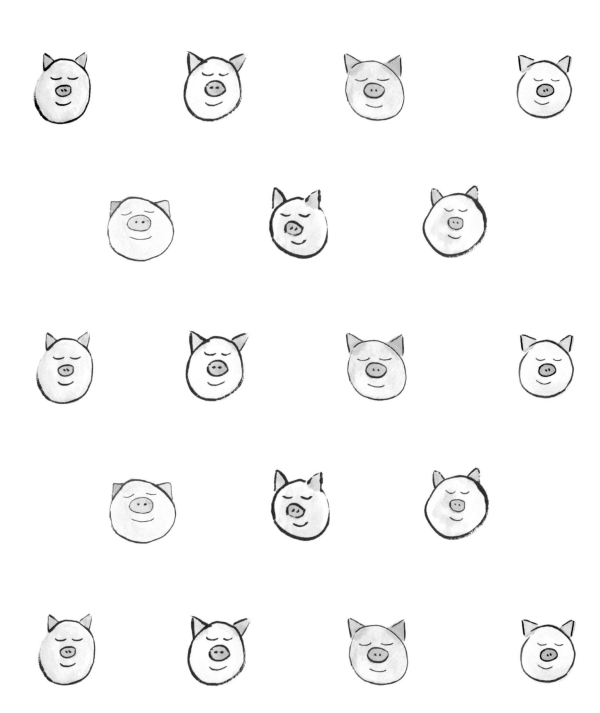

Made in the USA
Monee, IL
23 January 2021